T0353864

Where Did You Go?

RHODA WHITFIELD

WestBow Press books may be ordered through booksellers or by contacting:

WestBow Press
A Division of Thomas Nelson & Zondervan
1663 Liberty Drive
Bloomington, IN 47403
www.westbowpress.com
1 (866) 928-1240

ISBN: 978-1-5127-3757-8 (sc)
ISBN: 978-1-5127-3756-1 (e)

Library of Congress Control Number: 2016905599

Print information available on the last page.

WestBow Press rev. date: 5/11/2016

WESTBOW
PRESS®
A DIVISION OF THOMAS NELSON
& ZONDERVAN

This book was presented to:

_____

Date:

_____

Dedication

This book is dedicated to our beloved son Jarred Sean Whitfield. He was called home to be with the Lord at the age of 31 after a 5 month fight with Kidney cancer. He is truly missed by his children (ages 12, 7 and 2), family and friends. However, we rest in our belief that we will see him again. Gone too soon................

Author's Notes

When a child is young, they learn to be separated from their parents or caregiver for a short period of time. They learn that mom or dad will return sometime later and they make the necessary adjustments because they know their parent will return sooner or later. In other words, the child will adjust to being separated from their parent because they come to recognize it as a temporary state of being.

But what happens when the parent of a child dies? What happens when the pattern of mom or dad leaving and returning is changed due to death? Adults must be careful to view death through the eyes of a child accustomed to their parent leaving, but also returning. When the adult begins to address death with a child that has lost one or both of their parents, it is important to understand that this type of separation must be explained to the child in terms of temporary, permanent and eternal separation.

However, even after a couple of days of separation from a parent, the child will begin to ask questions and even demonstrate distinct behavior issues which are often erratic and unpredictable. Those questions and behaviors are magnified upon the death of a deceased parent who no longer returns. The question that lingers for the child is "Where did he or she go?" This book has been designed to assist in answering that question.

It is my prayer that this book can serve as a tool to aid you in helping your child better understand death whether it came through illness or a sudden unexpected demise. In other words, it is my hope that through the use of this book you will be able to help your child better understand the separation from their parent and where their parent has gone.

"Unanswered Questions"

Author: Rhoda Whitfield

Where are you?

Where did you go?

I don't understand and I really want to know.

I saw you on yesterday, but you're gone today.

And every time I ask, no one will really say.

Why didn't you tell me you were going away?

Was it my fault that you left?

Did I do something wrong?

Where are you?

Can you please come back to stay?

I'm missing you dearly every day.

My sweet little one, you are too young to fully understand that life has taken a turn that no one was expecting.

None of us had any idea what was about to happen and change our lives forever. We were all together as a family and we loved each other dearly.

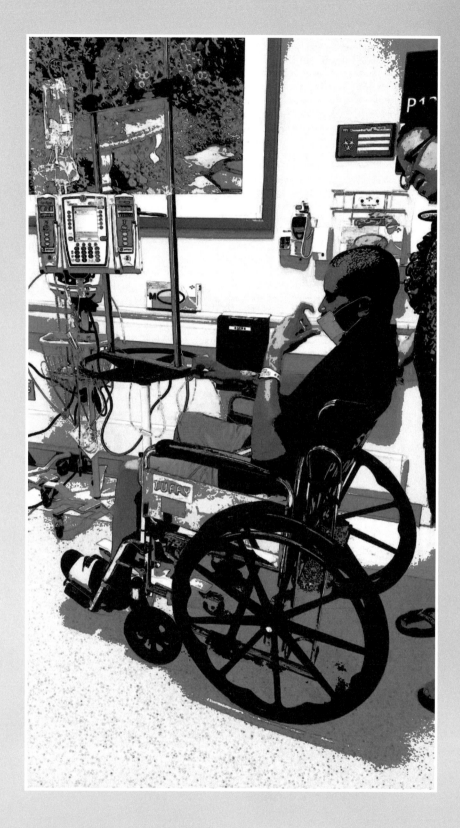

But one day Daddy became sick and was sent to the emergency room to have some test reviewed. It was then that we received the diagnosis none of us ever imagined. They said Daddy was sick and would need some special treatments.

It was hard for us to believe the doctors. So Mommy and Daddy traveled to Texas to seek a second opinion from a cancer research hospital. That is when they told us that the diagnosis about my health was correct.

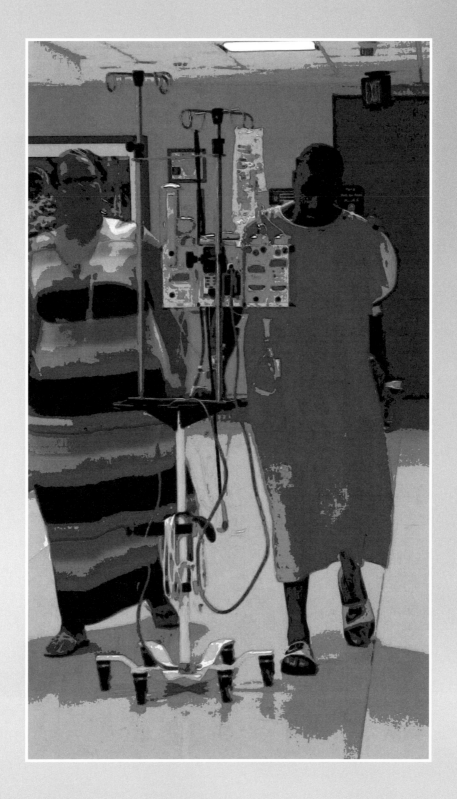

So I began having chemo treatments right away. These are treatments given to cancer patients to help kill the cancer cells.

Everything was going okay. I had no doubt that I would get well so I could continue to be with you and the rest of my family. However, Daddy was sick--- really sick, baby. Things didn't work out quite as we prayed. God took me to another home and gave me a new body. Now, I'm no longer in pain.

Tooka, I know you are missing me now. But, I truly miss you, your brothers and Mommy too.

Your smile and your laugh, I still can see.

In fact, I loved you from the beginning, before you were even born.

When God blessed Mommy and I with you, you were the apple of my eye.

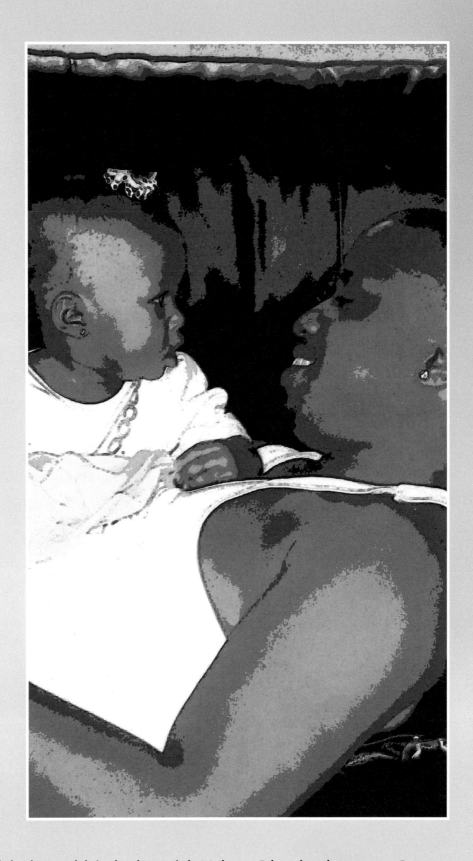

Daddy loved his baby girl. When I looked at you, I saw myself.

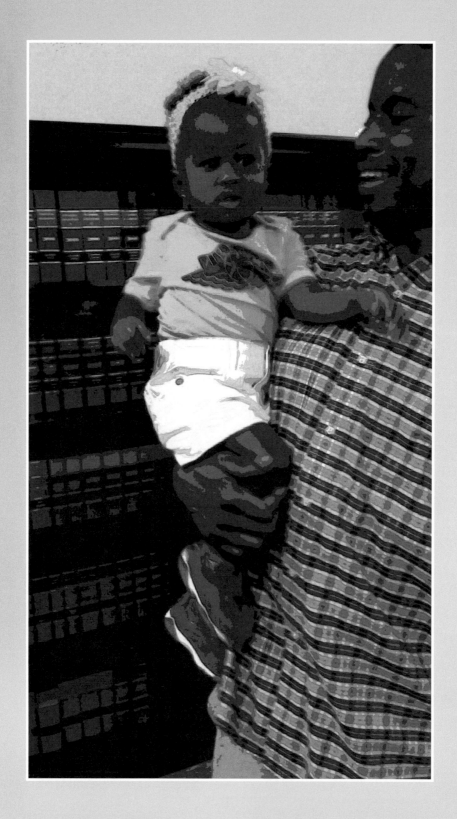

However, I know it's been a while since you've seen me and I know you are probably wondering where I am.

The boys on the other hand are older, and they may understand a little more than you as to where I am, and why you can no longer see and touch me.

But it will be a while before you really understand Tooka, that you can no longer find Daddy at home,

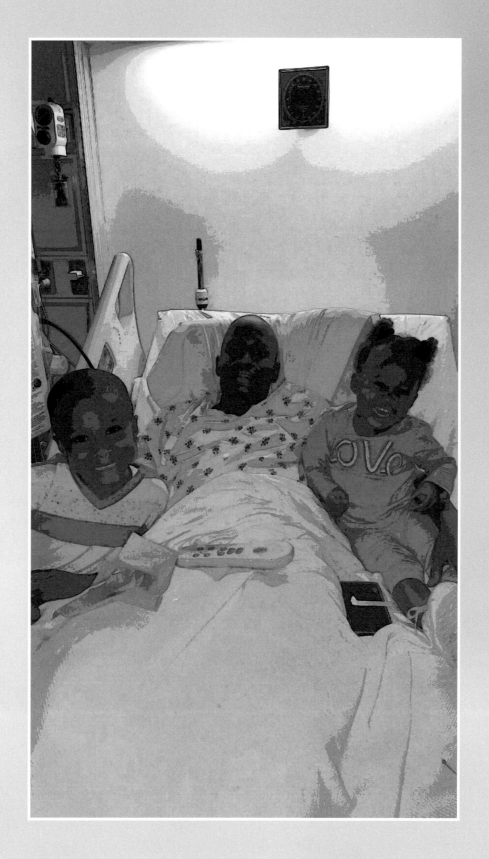

at the hospital,

or at church playing the drums.

Just know that I'm in a better place where I am no longer sick or in pain.

For now, I will have to be in your heart, our family's hearts and in your memories.

You will have to remember the good and fun times you had with Daddy--- The laughter we shared--- The memories we made.

Even though I won't share anymore birthdays and other holidays with you physically, I will be there in spirit at every occasion. Always remember that Daddy loved you. You will always be in my heart and I will always be in yours.

Although I'm not with you physically to see you grow up every day into the beautiful young lady I know you will be, know that Daddy will celebrate every success you experience from heaven.

So make me proud and I promise it will make me smile down from heaven to you.

I know our time together was short, but God has a way to help you to remember me, and the love I had for you.

In time, you will understand my departure better and I am so thankful that you, Mommy and your brothers have good support from....

Grandma and Papa will always love and be there for you.

And you all can depend on Tee Tee too!

You can definitely rely on Nana and Papa, who are never too busy to be there for any of you.

In fact, Tooka I can rest in peace knowing that my family has a super support system not just with the immediate family, but you have support throughout the whole family.

But, I have one request of you and your brothers. That all of you take care and surround Mommy in my absence. Cover Mommy with a lot of love because she loves all of you, but she needs each of you more than ever.

Holidays are going to be rough and different. But they still can be enjoyed as long as you are surrounded by family.

Don't worry about ever being alone. Remember, I am not there in my body, but my spirit will always be watching over you and the rest of the family from heaven.

So, Tooka - Daddy's sweet little one, whenever you wonder where I am, just know my old body is asleep down there with you and the family.

But if you look at the sky toward the heavens, that's where you will find me. I'm in heaven with Jesus.

Hey Tooka, I see you made it! Give Daddy a big smile. Say cheese!

That's my girl – you're the best little girl in the whole wide world. Always remember I love you all.

Develop your web story like Tooka

What loved one did you lose?

_____

Tooka lost her father to cancer.

What did you lose your loved one

to? _____

Insert your favorite picture of your loved one.

When you miss your loved one, what should you do?

_____

Complete the sentence.

My _____ loves me and I love my _____.

Insert a picture of you and your loved one at your youngest age.

Insert a picture of you and your loved one at your oldest age.

Tooka has two brothers. How many siblings do you have?

_____

Insert a picture of you when you were celebrating your birthday and your loved one was still with you.

Insert a picture of yourself when you were a baby

**Insert a picture where you were laughing
or playing with your loved one.**

39

Why can't you see and touch your loved one anymore?

_____

Where will you keep the memory of your loved one?

_____

Because your loved one is no longer here physically,

you should work hard to make them

_____

Insert a picture of Grandma and Papa or Grandma or Papa

Insert a picture of an aunt or uncle you believe you can depend on.

Insert a picture of your last holiday together with your loved one.

Who's watching over you now?

_____

Complete the sentence

_____ is in _____ with _____.

Remember it's okay to cry and miss your loved one.

Focus on all the good times and memories

that you made with them day to day.

Hold tight to those memories and never let them go.

Printed in the United States
By Bookmasters